Dr. Jekyll and Mr Hyde

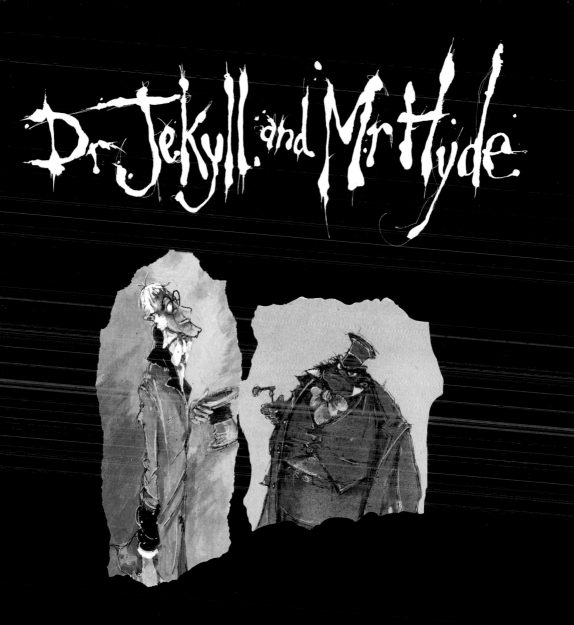

Adapted and Illustrated by

Chris Mould

OXFORD
UNIVERSITY PRESS

The Door

Mr Utterson the lawyer and his friend, Mr Richard Enfield, seldom spoke and found little in common on their Sunday walks. Yet they enjoyed these outings.

One of these rambles led them through a busy quarter of London. A sinister looking building butted outward into the street. There was but one door. Mr Enfield pointed.

'Did you ever see that door before?' he asked. 'It brings to mind a very strange tale.'

'I was returning home one night,' continued Enfield, 'when I saw a young girl, running, and a small man, lurching along. At the corner they collided and the man trampled over the girl. The family demanded a hundred pounds to avoid a scene and the man agreed to pay. But where do you think he went to get the money? That very door, sir.'

'Do you know the man's name?' asked Utterson.

'Edward Hyde,' replied Enfield. 'A detestable man.'

'That is my friend Dr Jekyll's house,' whispered Mr Utterson, uneasily.

The Search for Mr Hyde

That evening Mr Utterson was troubled. From his safe he took Dr Jekyll's will: in the case of the death of Jekyll all his possessions were to pass to his friend Hyde; in the case of his disappearance, Hyde should step into Jekyll's place. Who was Hyde?

Mr Utterson sought out his friend Dr Lanyon.

'We are Henry Jekyll's oldest friends,' began Mr Utterson.

'Quite so,' agreed Dr Lanyon. 'Though I seldom see him now.'

'Did you ever come across a friend of his named Hyde?'

'No,' was the reply.

That night, in bed, Enfield's tale unfolded over and over again in Utterson's head. In his nightmare he tried to see Hyde's face, but saw only the dark creatures of his imagination.

He began to haunt the doorway, morning, noon, and night, hoping to catch sight of Hyde.

At last his patience was rewarded. One frosty night, a small, odd-looking man approached as Utterson hid in the shadows. He drew a small key from his pocket. Utterson stepped out. 'Hyde, I think.'

Hyde recoiled in horror. 'That is my name. What do you want?'

'I am a friend of Dr Jekyll. May I come in?'

'He is not at home now,' cried Hyde, angered. Then he lowered his tone. 'Perhaps it is as well we have met.' He gave the lawyer his address, unlocked the door, and disappeared into the house.

Mr Utterson made his way to the front door of the house. Poole, the butler, admitted him. 'I'm afraid Dr Jekyll is out, sir,' he said.

'But Mr Hyde is here?' asked Utterson.

'Yes, sir. He has access at all times, through the laboratory.'

Utterson left, turning the will over in his mind. If Hyde knows about the will, he may grow impatient to inherit, he thought.

One evening after dinner, a fortnight later, Mr Utterson was sitting by the fire with Dr Jekyll.

'I've been wanting to speak to you about your will,' said Utterson.

'I know you never approved,' said Jekyll, uneasily.

'I approve even less, now I've seen Hyde. And I've heard a terrible story about him.'

'The moment I choose I can be rid of him,' Jekyll explained. 'If you knew everything, you would stand by my will. You must promise.'

And Utterson did so, but with a heavy heart.

The Carew Murder

Almost a year later, a crime startled the whole of London. A maidservant, living alone, looked out of her bedroom window at about eleven in the evening. She saw an elderly man walking along the lane and a smaller man walking towards him.

She recognized the smaller man as Mr Hyde, a friend of her master, Dr Jekyll. Suddenly Mr Hyde attacked the elderly man, and clubbed him to the ground with his stick. At this, the maid fainted.

At two o'clock she came to, and called the police, who found half of the stick next to the dead body. The next morning Mr Utterson identified the body as Sir Danvers Carew. He also saw the stick, and recognized it as one that he had given to Dr Jekyll. He and a policeman went immediately to Hyde's address.

They searched the house, and behind a door they found the other half of the stick. Proof that Hyde was their man.

A woman answered the door.
'Mr Hyde lives here, but he's not at home. He has not been home since last night.'

The Letter

Late that afternoon Utterson went to
visit Dr Jekyll. Poole showed him to the
laboratory. Jekyll sat there,
looking ill.

'Have you heard the news?'
asked Utterson.

'I have, and I swear that
I am done with Hyde. He's
sent me a letter, which I
wish you to keep.'

Utterson read the letter. It seemed to indicate Hyde's guilt,
and gave an assurance that he would not return.

'It was handed in at the door this morning,' said Jekyll.

'About your will,' said Utterson. 'Was it Hyde's idea?'

Jekyll nodded.

'Hyde meant to murder you, Jekyll. For your money.'

Utterson asked Poole about the letter as he left.

'I know nothing about a letter,' claimed Poole.

Utterson showed the letter to Mr Guest, a handwriting expert.

'It's an odd hand,' said Guest. He then took an old letter from Dr Jekyll, and placed it next to Hyde's.

'Why do you compare them?' asked Utterson.

'There is a great resemblance, only Hyde's writing is strangely sloped.'

'We must not speak of this,' said Utterson as he put the letter into his safe. Was Jekyll forging letters for the murderer, he wondered?

Rewards were offered, but it appeared that Hyde had disappeared for good. Now that his evil influence was gone, Dr Jekyll became himself again.

Utterson, Lanyon, and Jekyll rekindled their friendship, but suddenly Jekyll confined himself to the house once more. Utterson visited Lanyon and found him very ill.

'I have had a terrible shock. I am doomed,' he said. 'I am done with Jekyll. I wish to hear no more of him.'

Back at home, Utterson wrote to Jekyll. Why was he excluded from the house? What had caused the rift with Lanyon? A mysterious reply came the next day.

From now on, wrote Jekyll, I must live in seclusion. I am still your friend, but my door is shut to you.

Hyde was gone, but questions still remained unanswered. Shortly after, Dr Lanyon died.

After the funeral, Utterson sat at home, holding a letter from Lanyon. 'For the hands of J. G. Utterson alone.' Inside was a second letter. 'Not to be opened until the death or disappearance of Dr Henry Jekyll.'

What could this mean?

The following Sunday, Mr Utterson and Mr Enfield happened to pass the door once again.

'Well,' said Enfield. 'We shall see no more of Hyde.'

'I hope not,' replied Utterson. 'But I am still worried about Jekyll.' The two men stepped into the court.

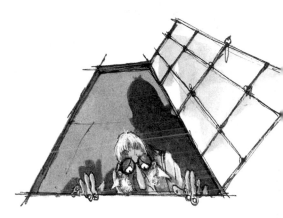

They could see Jekyll through a window.

'Are you well, Jekyll?' called Utterson.

'No, I am very low,' he replied.

Then a look of terror clouded Jekyll's face. They caught only a glimpse and then the window was pulled shut. The two men left the courtyard in silence.

The Last Night

One evening, Poole came to visit Mr Utterson.

'Something is wrong, Mr Utterson. Please come to the house and see for yourself.'

When they reached the house, Poole knocked at Jekyll's door.
'Go away!' said Jekyll.

'Did you notice how his voice is different?' gasped Poole. 'I have been to the chemist several times for medicine, but he says it isn't pure. Last time I saw him, he was wearing a mask!'

'Maybe he has an illness that has changed him,' said Utterson.

'But, sir, he was short. My master is tall and finely built.'

'Then poor Henry has been killed by Mr Hyde,' said Utterson. 'Let us break down the door.'

They did so. There, on the floor, lay the body of Hyde. On the desk lay Jekyll's will, redrawn in favour of Utterson. There was also a note from Jekyll. 'Go and read Lanyon's letter. Then read my confession.'

Dr Lanyon's Story

Utterson held Dr Lanyon's letter and began to read:

*On 9th January I received a letter from Dr Jekyll.
This is how the letter began:*

Dear Lanyon,
   Although we have differed
on scientific matters, I must
still ask a great favour of
you.

   The letter instructed me to
go to Jekyll's house that night.
We should remove a drawer
from his desk and I should take
it back to my house. A man
would appear at midnight to
collect it.

I felt sure my friend was insane, yet I did as he asked. There were powders and a container of liquid in the drawer.

At midnight a small, ugly man appeared at my door. It was Hyde. He sprang to the drawer and drank the liquid with some of the powders. Suddenly his features altered, and before me stood Henry Jekyll.

Hastie Lanyon

Jekyll and Hyde were the same person! It seemed inconceivable, yet it answered every question. Utterson now turned to Dr Jekyll's statement.

Dr Jekyll's Story

I was born rich and had every hope of a successful life. But as well as desiring public respect, I also wished to enjoy life's pleasures. I therefore created two lives for myself—the pleasure-seeking rake and the gentlemanly doctor.

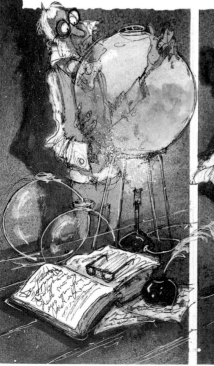

I wondered if it were possible to really separate myself, and through my scientific study I succeeded. One night, I drank my liquid . . .

I looked in my mirror and saw Edward Hyde's evil, yet welcoming, face for the first time. I returned to my laboratory and drank the mixture once more, becoming Jekyll again. I could lead a double life!

I suffered pangs . . . a grinding in my bones . . . and then youth, brightness, happiness, and wickedness boiled inside me.

I took and furnished a house for Hyde, and told my servants that he could have access to my own house at any time. Then I drew up my will in case of any mishap.

While I was Hyde, Jekyll's conscience slept. Hyde was guilty, not Jekyll, of the trampling of a child.

One night I went to bed as Jekyll, but I awoke as Hyde. How could this happen without taking the drug? I feared that Hyde had a strong hold on me, and resolved not to take the drug for two months.

But in a moment of weakness I drank it—and Hyde came out again.

It was on this night that I met Carew and killed him with my stick. I realized I must protect Jekyll and made haste to Hyde's house and removed all evidence of a link between Jekyll and Hyde. But in my panic I forgot the broken stick.

Dr Jekyll was safe, but Hyde was now a murderer. I remained as Jekyll. But this could not last for long.

I was in Regent's Park when I found I had become Hyde. I could not reach my drugs! If I tried to enter my house I would be arrested. I went to a hotel, and wrote to Lanyon and Poole, instructing them about the drawer.

I transformed myself before Lanyon's eyes and it proved too much for him. I went home, but I was not safe anywhere. I could transform at any moment. Poole fetched me chemicals but they no longer worked.

I am finishing this statement under the last of my potions. This is the last time I shall see my face in the glass. I hope I will have the courage to finish Hyde off. I lay down my pen, and bring to an end the unhappy life of Henry Jekyll.

OXFORD
UNIVERSITY PRESS

Great Clarendon Street, Oxford OX2 6DP

Oxford University Press is a department of the University of Oxford.
It furthers the University's objective of excellence in research, scholarship,
and education by publishing worldwide in

Oxford New York

Athens Auckland Bangkok Bogotá Buenos Aires
Cape Town Chennai Dar es Salaam Delhi Florence Hong Kong Istanbul
Karachi Kolkata Kuala Lumpur Madrid Melbourne Mexico City Mumbai
Nairobi Paris São Paulo Shanghai Singapore Taipei Tokyo Toronto Warsaw

with associated companies in Berlin Ibadan

Oxford is a registered trade mark of Oxford University Press
in the UK and in certain other countries

Copyright © Chris Mould 2000
The moral rights of the author have been asserted

Database right Oxford University Press (maker)

First published 2000
First published in this edition 2001

British Library Cataloguing in Publication Data available

ISBN 0 19 272502 5

1 3 5 7 9 10 8 6 4 2

Printed in Malaysia